This book belongs to.....................

To Tom, Ella and Louis

First published in 2009 by Child's Play (International) Ltd
Ashworth Road, Bridgemead, Swindon SN5 7YD

Distributed in USA by Child's Play Inc
250 Minot Avenue, Auburn, Maine 04210

Distributed in Australia by Child's Play Australia Pty Ltd
Unit 10/20 Narabang Way
Belrose, NSW 2085

ISBN 978-1-84643-287-3

Printed and bound in China

1 3 5 7 9 10 8 6 4 2

A catalogue record of this book is available from the British Library

www.childs-play.com

I Told You So!

Sarah Arnold

Child's Play®

Nursey, Tom and Ella were going to the park.

Nursey's eyesight was terrible, and she bumped into everything. Where *had* she put her glasses?

Inside the park there was a freezing wind,
so Nursey buttoned up Ella's coat and wrapped
a nice warm scarf around her neck.

As she did so, a cold little robin in a nearby tree
saw Tom in his pram, warm and snug.
Quickly, it slipped under the covers.

"Nursey!" Ella cried.
"There's a robin in Tom's pram!"

"Don't be ridiculous, Darling," said Nursey.
"I can't see a robin."

They pushed the pram up the hill,
and Nursey stopped to admire the view.

As she did so,
a cold little rabbit
saw Tom in his pram,
warm and snug.
Quickly, it hopped
under the covers.

"Nursey!" Ella cried.
"There's a rabbit in Tom's pram!"
"Don't be ridiculous, Darling,"
said Nursey. "I can't see a rabbit."

When they arrived at the café,
Nursey went to get a cup of coffee.

Whilst she was talking to Mr Dog, a cold little duck
waddling by saw Tom in his pram, warm and snug.
Quickly, it flew up and dived under the covers.

"Nursey!" cried Ella. "Now there's
a duck in Tom's pram!"
"Nonsense, Ella," replied Nursey.
"I can't see a duck."

Nursey drank her hot coffee and the steam
rose up in front of her bad eyes.
Just at that moment, a cold little billy goat
tripping by saw Tom in his pram, warm and snug.
Quickly, it jumped up under the covers.

"Nursey! Nursey!
Now there's a billy goat
in Tom's pram!"

"Goodness me!" said Nursey.
"What an imagination
you have, Ella!
I think you must be
sickening for something.
We should go home
right away!"

Nursey pushed the pram up the hill, but the pram
was very heavy and she had to push very hard.

"Goodness, Tom!" exclaimed Nursey, as she stopped
to rub her sore back. "You are so heavy!
What have you been eating?"

At that moment, a cold little wolf who was also very hungry saw Tom in his pram, warm and snug - and very tasty-looking! Quickly, it slipped under the covers.

All at once, there was a noise of scuffling and chomping and licking of lips coming from the pram! Nursey cocked her head to one side, and wondered what the strange noise could be.

"Nursey!" Ella cried. "Tom's become a wolf!"
"Nonsense, Darling," Nursey replied. "But I must say,
he's a funny colour! I wish I could find my glasses and
have a better look at him."

"Here they are, Nursey!" said Ella.
She slipped the glasses onto Nursey's nose.

Nursey pulled back the covers
and saw that in place of Tom
there was a very, very fat little wolf!

Nursey screamed at the top of her voice. She showed all her snaggly old teeth, which frightened the wolf so much...

... that he let out
an enormous
hiccup and belch!
Out of his mouth flew...

the rabbit,

...the robin,

the duck...

...and the billy goat!

But there was still no sign of little Tom!

So Nursey grabbed the wolf, who still looked rather fat,
and shook him by the ankles until Tom fell out.

Nursey threw the wolf as far as she could
before taking little Tom and Ella home.

Then she had to lie down on the sofa with a bag of frozen peas on her head!

And Ella said...

"I *told* you so!"